Santa ~~Claus~~ Bruce

Ryan T. Higgins

SCHOLASTIC INC.

For Joanna

ISBN 978-1-338-71586-6

12 11 10 9 8 7 6 5 4 3 2 1   20 21 22 23 24 25

Printed in the U.S.A   40

This edition first printing, November 2020

This book is set in Macarons/Fontspring with hand-lettering by Ryan T. Higgins.
Designed by Tyler Nevins.
Illustrations were created using scans of treated clayboard for textures, graphite, ink, and Photoshop.

Bruce was a bear
who did not like the holidays.

He used to stay in bed all winter long
and skip right through the whole business.

This is going to be a great
Christmas! No migrating!
No hibernating! Just family.

HONK

But his family wanted
to enjoy a cozy, snow-filled
Christmas together.

So Bruce was awake.

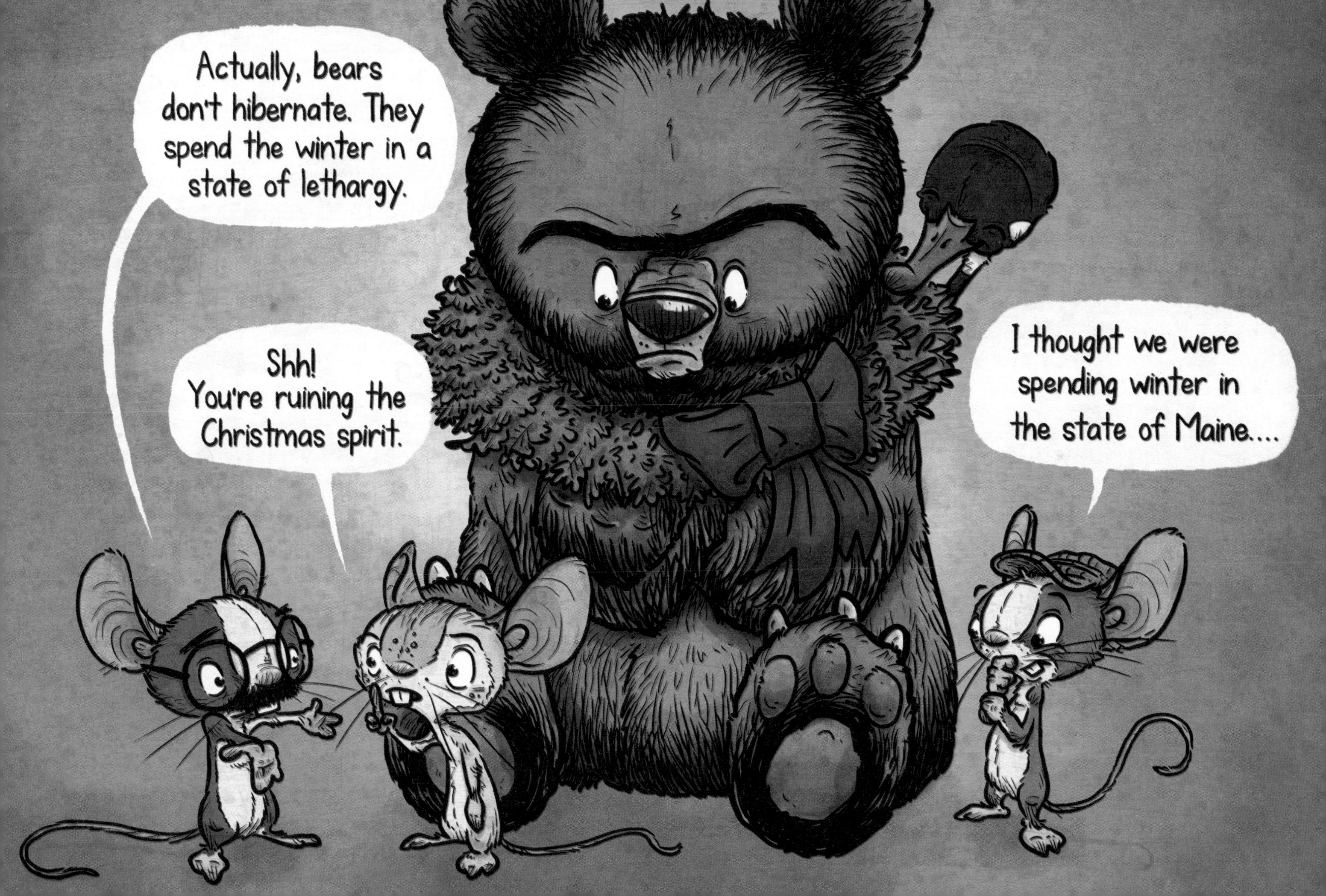

The geese had decked the halls.

The mice made lots of eggnog.

The holiday season was going to be filled with fun and cheer.

Bruce did not like fun.

Bruce did not like cheer.

Bruce did not like fun *or* cheer.

Bruce also did not like being cold. Which is why he started wearing long underwear and a warm hat.

And then it happened . . . again.

A case of mistaken identity.

Bruce did not like mistaken identities.

Bruce decided to ignore the problem
until it went away.

It did not.

It got worse.

Soon word spread,

I want ninety-nine red balloons for Christmas!

For Christmas, I want world peace.

and all the little critters of the forest wanted to visit Santa Bruce . . .

Finally, they all went home and
Bruce could grumble in peace and quiet.

But not for long . . .

KNOCK
KNOCK
KNOCK

. . . because all the parents wanted to thank Bruce for his Christmas spirit.

Bruce tried to tell them that he didn't have any.

Bah humbug!

That's when Thistle
made an announcement.

Bruce wants to say
you're welcome! AND what's
more, Santa Bruce is going to
deliver presents to all of your
kids tonight!

And with that, the parents left,
shouting out with glee.

Bruce did not like glee.

Finally, Bruce headed to bed.
The mice had other ideas.

But what about getting ready for your big night?

Yeah, what about the children?!

Bruce put his foot down.

But the mice were persistent.

The geese were helpful.

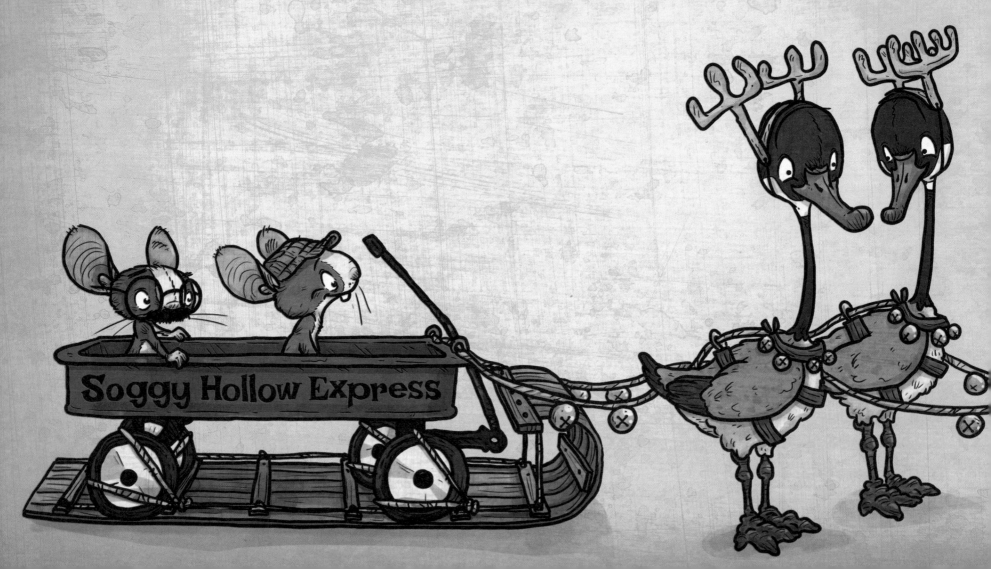

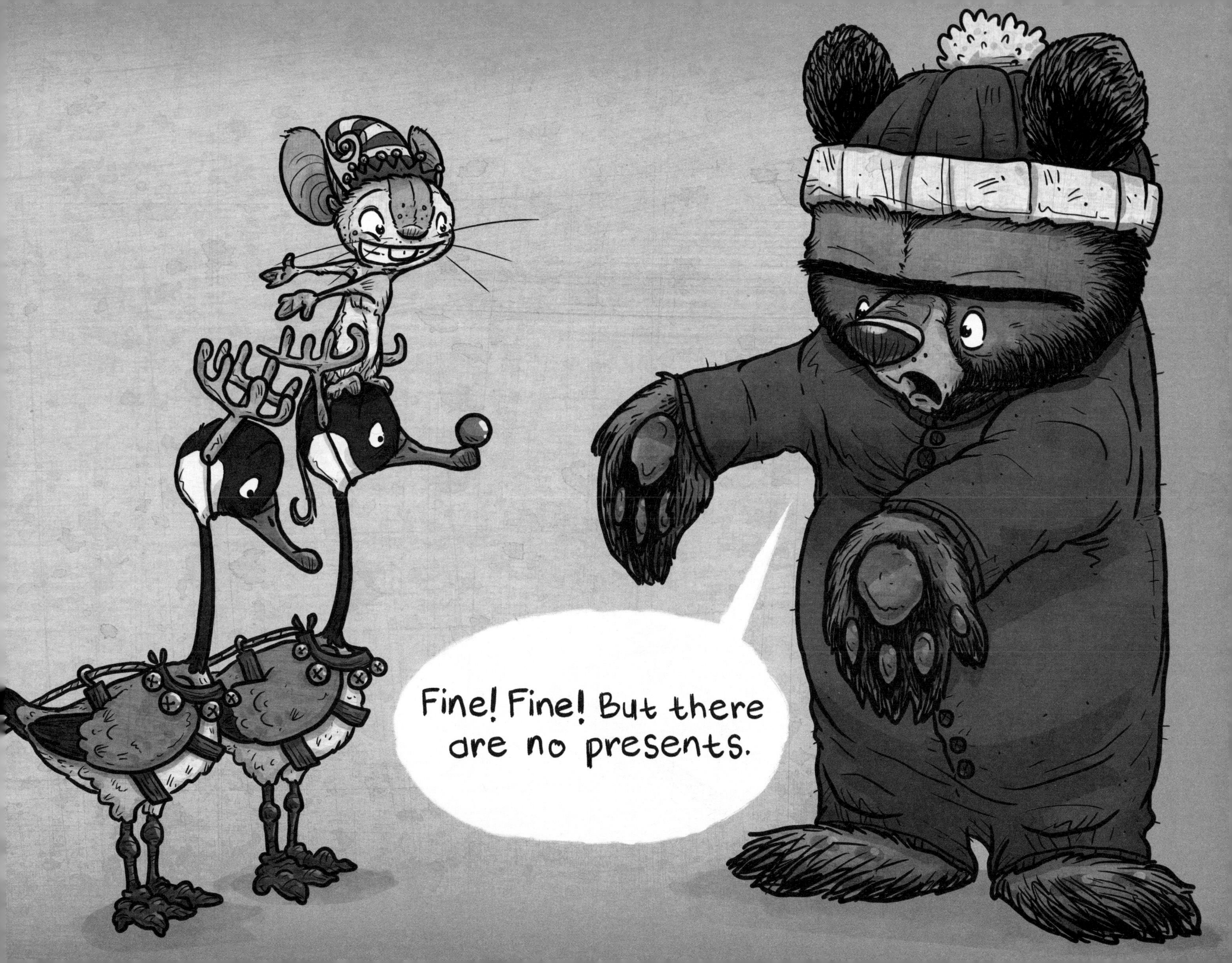
Fine! Fine! But there are no presents.

And everyone was ready.

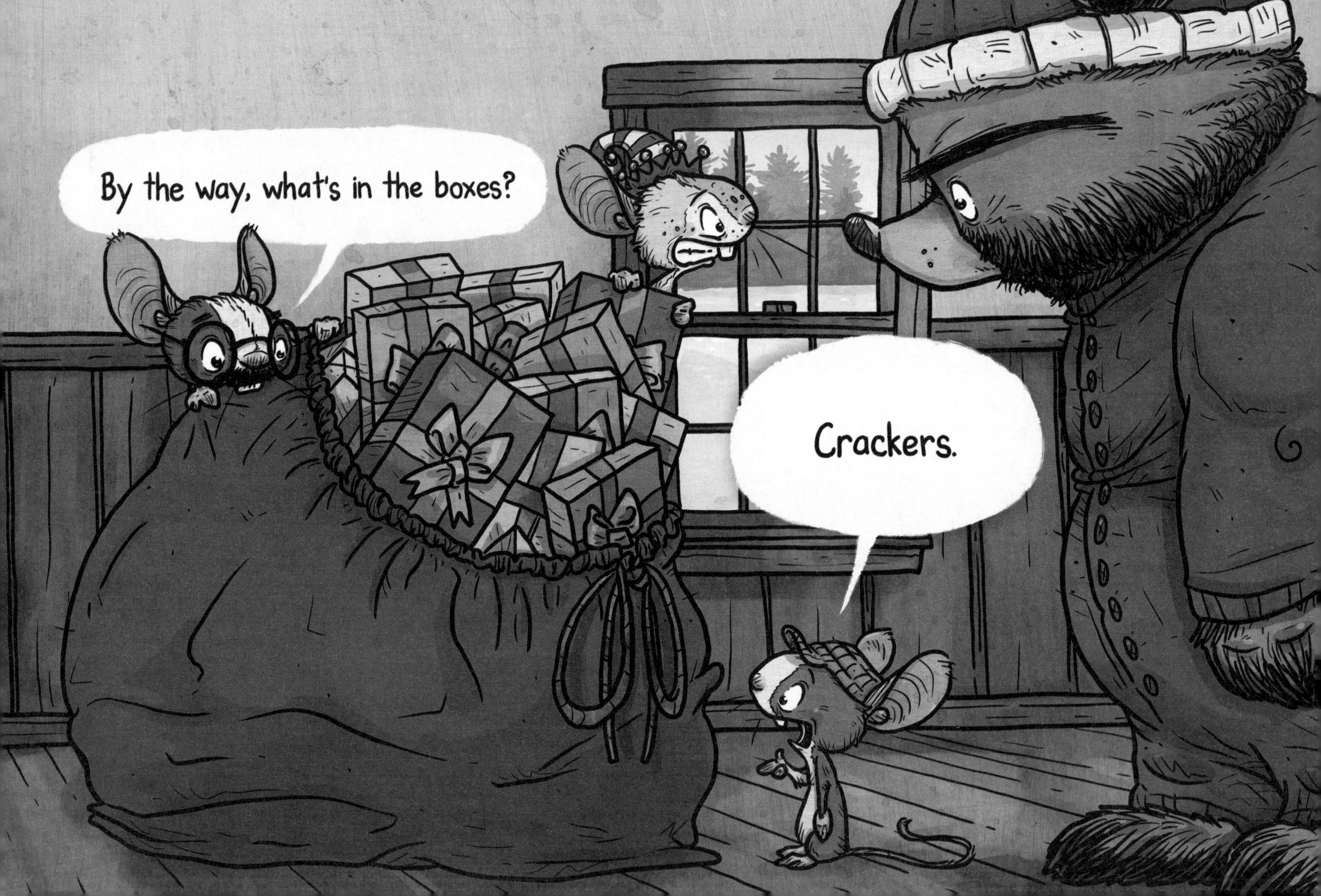

I'm still not going.
Pleeeeeease?! All you have to do is sit in the sled. We'll give you chocolate eggs....

Finally, the grumpy old bear agreed to be Santa Bruce for one night.

And everyone was very happy.

Being Santa Bruce
was not an easy job.

And by the time Santa Bruce finally finished, the early morning light was creeping over a white Christmas.

Hollow Express

As all the critters of the forest awoke, they found presents waiting for them from Santa Bruce.

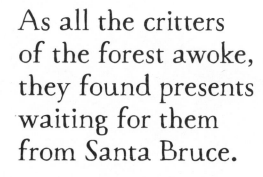

Crackers!

Bruce had spread the spirit of
Christmas all over the forest,
and brought everyone happiness.

MERRY CHRISTMAS,
BRUCE!!

Bruce did not like happiness.
He liked sleeping.

But Bruce's bed would have to wait.